Buford Bee and the Little Dogwood Tree

by Maxine Sweeney

Cattail Creek Books
Elizabeth City, North Carolina

Maxine Sweeney

Dedication

For Laura and all
the Sweeney Grandchildren

Sweeney, Maxine.
    Buford Bee and the Little Dogwood Tree / by Maxine Sweeney. --
        1st ed.
    p.cm.
    ISBN: 0-9666142-2-4
    ISBN: 0-9666142-3-2
    SUMMARY: Four stories about the woodland hero Buford Bee,
    who rescues a dogwood tree, saves a group of firefly dancers with
    his friend Freddie Frog, enjoys the party put on by the frog chorus
    and helps reunite a mother turtle with her little daughter.

    1. Bees--Juvenile fiction.   2. Trees--Juvenile fiction.
    3. Fireflies--Juvenile fiction.   4. Frogs--Juvenile fiction.
    5. Turtles--Juvenile fiction.   I. Title.

    PZ7.S97428Buf 2000

When Buford awakened in the morning he tried to get his wife Miranda to go flying with him. She just sighed and said, "I don't feel like flying, Buford. I just don't want to go flying."

"Well, I do," said Buford. "I'm going to fly over everything in sight. I'm going to fly upside down and rightside up. I'm going to fly above the trees and smell the wildflowers. Then I'm going to lie down on a cloud and take a nap. It's such a special day."

So Buford flew up in the air and laughed and played in the clouds until he got tired.

Looking around, he spied his friend, the little dogwood tree. The tree looked even more inviting for a nap than the clouds, so Buford flew over, found the perfect place for a rest and closed his eyes. He had just dozed off when he heard a sad sound and someone say, "Oh oh—oh my!" Buford got down from his perch and said, "Little tree, are you sick?"

"Well, yes," said the little dogwood tree. "Someone tied a tight wire around my waist, Buford. It will get tighter and tighter as I grow, and then I just don't know what will happen to me."

Buford thought and thought.

As he looked toward the fields, he saw Farmer Brown working with his young son packing tomatoes.

"He'll help me. I know he will," thought Buford.

"I know how to get his attention. I'll ask Hennie Hummingbird to buzz him and fly away, and buzz him again and again until he follows her."

Miss Hennie was glad to help, so she flew over and got Farmer Brown to follow her.

Farmer Brown soon found the little tree, and with his snips he cut the wire and saved Buford's friend. But that's not all of this story.

The little tree was so happy to be free of the wire that she wanted to reward Buford and Farmer Brown. She had her bird friends drop seeds on Buford's island home and around the farmhouse where Farmer Brown lived.

Today many beautiful dogwood trees grow. They flower and perfume the air on Buford's island home. Buford will always remember his little friend, the dogwood tree.

It was late one afternoon when Buford found Freddie Frog sitting still on his lily pad with a curious expression on his face, humming a little tune.

What you doing, Fred? asked Buford. He flew to a large leaf and settled down for a talk with Freddie, but Freddie was intently watching the woods near the creek.

"Something strange is going on over there, Buf. Every night about this time, at dusk or when it's dark, some lights come on over there in a straight line and start moving. I hear sounds, too, like music. I wish I knew what was going on."

Buford was getting interested. "Let's go over there and hide behind some flowers and see what those lights are all about."

It was a very surprised Buford and Freddie who first saw the strange goings-on beside the creek.

Large elephant ears were secured so they wouldn't move. Balanced on one was a graceful little figure, Miss Fiona Firefly.

Miss Fiona led the row of fireflies that appeared from above, dancing a lovely ballet dance. They landed, all lighting up at once, followed by another row of dancers. The night was bright with the beautiful sight of lights and dancing fireflies.

"Well, what do you know about that?" said Buford. "I had no idea they had been practicing anything so beautiful. Maybe they'll let us come every night and watch them dance.

So they asked, and everything was fine until one evening some little children also came to watch the lights.

The next night the children came again and sat down to watch the fireflies dance. Sometimes the fireflies all leaped at once in a shower of lights, looking for all the world like the human Fourth of July fireworks.

"I would like to catch some of them to light my play house," said a little girl, "but I don't want to hurt them, so we'll need some screen wire for the top of our jar so they can breathe."

The little children brought some screen wire and then began to run and catch the dancers and put them in the jar they had brought.

Buford and Freddie were watching and wondering how to go about rescuing their little friends.

Freddie said, "Buford, you always think of everything, but this time I'm going to solve the problem. I'll get my frog chorus to hop over to their playhouse. We'll get on all four corners of the screen wire and pull and tug until the wire comes off and our friends can get out."

And that is what they did. Buford was very happy to have someone else helping him solve the problems of his woodland friends.

On any pretty night the fireflies are still dancing and lighting up the night. Buford still talks to his friends the frogs about the time they watched the midnight dancers.

Freddie was singing when Buford flew over the creek to talk to the firefly dancers. He flew close to listen and had to laugh as it was a silly song that Freddie made up.

"I think that I will never see
A suit as pretty as a bee's
With all those stripes in gold and black
And little buttons down the back
Oh, I'd rather be a bee than me.

My green suit doesn't fit the bill
It makes me look old—over the hill
I wish I could be gold and black too
Then I'd rather be me than you."

Buford for once was speechless with laughter, but he had to come over with a great idea to try out on Freddie and could hardly wait to tell him about it.

"Freddie, you know, if the fireflies can entertain the woodland creatures, why can't we? You have your frog chorus, the birds have their different songs and trills, and if all the bees flapped their wings at once and stomped their feet, we could sound like whirs and drums. Why can't we have a Bee and Frog Entertainment Night?"

Freddie sat up straight, excited at the idea of his Frog Chorus being noticed. "It's a great idea, Buford. We will have honey cakes and honey soda. We will have wild strawberry pie and onion soup, salads and honeysuckle punch, and then the singing will begin."

So they began to plan, and the day and night of the party came at last. The stage was set and the Frog Chorus was seated, ready to go. Firefly dancers were lined up behind the bamboo screen ready to dance when a loud screeching noise sounded in the back row. Buford tiptoed around the side and looked right into the eyes of a big, brown ferocious-looking bear who he knew was about to eat all their refreshments.

What to do—what to do. He had to be brave, so he twirled his wings, threw out his chest and walked up to the bear.

"You are not invited to our party," he said. It was no sooner out of his mouth than he began to think of how mean he had been recently to Miss Butterfly. Buford suddenly was ashamed of himself. Buford did the right thing.

"Mr. Bear," he said, "I have not been nice to you because you have always stolen our honey. Well, now I know that you are hungry sometimes, so—we are inviting you to our play and party, and from now on you will find a honeycomb for yourself and your children in the woods behind Farmer Brown's barn."

"Let's forget all past ill will and let tonight be fun night, so get your children and come on in and join the fun."

Now Buford was all smiles again. Their great party was soon the talk of Cattail Creek. And guess what? The end of it was best of all— a dance by Mr. Bear and singing and dancing by the Cattail Creek frogs.

The next day was bright and sunny when Buford opened his eyes.
The first thing he thought was that the hives needed to be tended.
Buford told Miranda that he and the worker bees were flying to the
vacant lot next to Farmer Brown's farm. They were going to gather
nectar to make more honey for the hives.

The wildflowers that lived there had promised to let them have
lots of nectar, so the bees got their little pails and flew away to work.

As they flew over the narrow road, Buford could see his good friend Tillie Turtle. She and her baby Tiny were waiting beside the road for a safe time to cross over on their way to the creek.

As Buford flew over to visit, he heard Tillie say to her little one, "Now you wait until I tell you that you can cross the road. You could be hurt if you're not very careful."

But Tiny was anxious to swim in the creek. She raced ahead of her mother into the middle of the road.

At first Tillie was mad with Tiny, but then a bicycle appeared in the distance. A little girl was pedaling as fast as she could. She stopped just in time when she saw the baby turtle.

The little girl got down on her knees. She looked at Tiny and said, "Oh, you are so cute, I'm going to take you home with me and fix a nice tub for you. I'm going to fill it with dirt and moss. Then I'll put in some pieces of wood so you can rest and sleep. You can play sometimes on my windowsill in the sunlight. You'll love it and I'll be ever so good to you."

Buford looked at Tillie, and Tillie looked at Buford. He knew she heard the little girl, and he saw tears begin to fall down Tillie's face.

"She has my baby—how will I ever get her back to live with me?" Tillie said.

Buford was sad. He thought and thought. Then he said, "You are not to worry, Tillie. I'm going to follow that bicycle and see where that little girl is going to take Tiny."

Buford flew off close behind them. He was very surprised to see the little girl turn her bicycle toward the creek where Tillie had been going in the first place. Buford flew close to the girl's ear when he saw that she was talking to Tiny.

"I've been thinking, little turtle," he heard her say, "Your mother may be looking for you. How sad she would be if you came home with me. I'm going to take you down to the creek and leave you with the grown-up turtles on the big log. I'll ask them to look after you until your mother finds you."

"Your baby is safe and down by the creek," he said, "but you know, Tillie, Miss Tiny needs to learn a lesson. I think she learned one today, but just in case she didn't, I think you might want to tap her a time or two so she'll remember. You'll feel better and she'll be wiser."

Then Buford smiled, and with a wave of his wings said good-bye to his turtle friend.

"You know, Miranda," he said, "there seem to be more and more problems for me to solve, or is it that I'm getting older?"